ANGELS ON ASSIGNMENT

Adventures on the Beach

by Nadine Helmuth Patton

ISBN-13: 978-1974644988
ISBN-10: 1974644987
Cover design by Ashley Burgess
Illustrations by Ashley Burgess

Hopeful Heart Resources
www.thehearteyes.com

Angels on Assignment series
Book 1 - Adventures on the Farm
Book 2 - Adventures on the Beach

Dedicated to
my grandchildren,
Asher
Sophie
Eli
Josslyn
Jacob

With special thanks to my cousin, Steven Helmuth, Sr. for his insight and helpful information on surfing. He's been surfing since 1975. Steven has surfed in 7 countries, Hawaii, California and all along the East Coast of the United States. He's been a finalist three times in the Eastern U.S. Surfing Association. His knowledge is fascinating to me, and anything that has been conveyed inaccurately in my writing is entirely my fault and not his.

Chapter 1

Ben grabbed his surfboard and walked as fast as he could towards the beach. The tide was coming in this morning, and he couldn't wait to catch some waves.

Ah, how he had missed the ocean. Living with Mom most of the year didn't allow him to come to the beach as often as he wanted, but the summer weeks with Dad would give him lots of time to practice his surfing skills.

Ben wished his twin sister, Bailey, would have come with him, but she wanted to sleep in. Ben knew she had some fears of the ocean and wondered how she would do at her summer surf camp.

He waved at Tony and Garth, who were already in the ocean. His heart beat faster, and he shivered as he stepped into the cold water. *I probably should have worn my wetsuit.*

There weren't many people on the seashore this early, and the fog was too thick to see the sun. Suddenly he saw the dolphins. A pair of them, gliding in graceful arches in and out of the waves right in front of him. Such beautiful creatures. He stood still for a moment to watch them.

"Hey, dude!" He heard Tony yell. "Waves are great. Get on out here!"

Ben picked up his board and headed out to where the waves were breaking. Although Ben couldn't see them, the angels that had always been with him were near. Yilt and Lontoo were keenly aware of the danger that morning and knew God had them on assignment.

Ben greeted his buddies and watched for a perfect wave. The wind was blowing offshore, and it made the waves look like glass tubes. He attached his leash and gripped the rails of his board. He watched for the wave he wanted and began to paddle towards it.

His first duck dive into the water brought him up to the peak of the wave. He jumped up on his board into a balanced position. It felt spectacular! That was his favorite word to describe surfing.

Riding on top of the waves was like nothing else he'd ever known. Ben had worked hard to become stronger and hoped to improve his skills this summer. Someday he wanted to compete.

The breaking waves were a perfect match for Ben's skills. But something in the water caught his attention. Before he could figure out that there was something wrong, the wave smacked into him. Hard. *Ouch, that hurt!*

He felt his body being pulled under and his brain couldn't think. His fingers touched something hard. His board. He reached for it and tried to grab it with both hands.

He struggled and kicked and finally surfaced. He sucked air in quickly, then felt his body being pulled under the water again.

The fear Ben felt made him think he was going to die. He wanted to pray, but he wasn't sure how. All Ben could think of was *God help me.*

He didn't know if God heard him, but a feeling of peace came to his mind and allowed his body to relax.

When he came to the surface again, the set of waves had passed, and the water was calm. He was thankful for the leash that tied his feet and his surfboard to each other. He floated toward the beach and was finally able to touch the sand with his feet. As he gasped for air, Tony and Garth were next to him.

Garth splashed water at him and laughed. "What was that all about, Ben? You forget how to part the waters?"

Ben was embarrassed. It was like a giant ugly Scoundrel of Humiliation lunged at his thoughts. He was still shaking from thinking he would die. Maybe he had forgotten his skills. Maybe he wasn't as good as he thought. His doubts allowed more Evil Scoundrels of Defeat and Insecurity to jump into his mind.

Ben felt jittery and wanted to quit and go home. Tony asked what happened. Ben shook his head. He wasn't sure, but he didn't want his friends to know how scared he was.

"You're shaking, dude!" Tony said, coming closer. He saw the fear in Ben's eyes. "Hey, it's okay. It's been quite a while since you've been out. Don't worry about it."

Ben's breathing began to calm down, and Tony's concern made him feel better.

"Did you see our dolphin friends? They seem to like being around us." Garth nodded toward the water, and suddenly Ben realized it had been the dolphins that had distracted him.

They had come really close and caught him off guard. *Had they hit the end of his board or had his focus shifted and caused him to lose his balance?* Ben wasn't sure. He'd have to be more cautious.

He wasn't as excited to head back to the waves, but he also knew it would be better if he faced his fears right away.

The rest of the morning he picked smaller waves and stayed closer to the shore. His friends kept yelling at him to come farther out and try the bigger waves, but Ben wasn't ready, and he chose to ignore their taunting.

He knew they practiced all year. They met when he had surfed before, and they sometimes sent him pictures of their latest tricks.

When the fog finally cleared and the tide was coming in, the boys decided to head back to the beach. Tony and Garth planned to meet the next day. Ben told them he didn't know if he could make it. He hung his head as he carried his surfboard back to the house.

As he came to the front porch, he saw their neighbor sweeping her sidewalk. Everyone called her 'Grins'. She waved and pointed to his surfboard. "How were the waves?"

Ben stopped to talk with her. He and Bailey had spent time with the folks next door last Christmas. They rode together in the Christmas parade and played games by the fireplace on cold days. He forgot they would be there in the summer.

"The waves were great," Ben told her. *Except for the first big one.* He was not happy about that moment and hoped he could forget it. He was frustrated at his lack of focus.

"Pops always loved surfing," she said. "I never learned how." Pops was her husband, and Ben loved riding in his convertible. He remembered Dad telling him they were retiring from their farm and moving to their beach house full time.

He wished there were kids living next door, but he was grateful he'd found a few friends on the island. He hated having his parents living in separate places. He still wasn't used to it.

"Our grandson will be visiting this summer. He arrives tomorrow. It would be fun to plan some events together." She seemed very excited.

That sounded good to Ben, and he gave her a thumbs-up. He wasn't sure Dad would have time for fun things, and Bailey would be busy with her camp.

Ben went into his house and found Bailey eating breakfast. *What a slowpoke. It was almost lunchtime.* Ben was ready to get the bikes out and ride over to the bay side of the Island. He didn't like being patient with his sister.

He didn't know why, but the morning had left him impatient and grumpy. Evil Scoundrels of Irritation kept poking at his thoughts and Ben was having a hard time not saying mean things. When Dad asked him about his morning of surfing, he grunted a fast 'okay' and headed for the shower.

Dad gave Bailey a questioning look, and she shrugged. "Who knows," she said. "Sometimes he's just cranky. I don't like his bad moods."

As soon as that popped out of her mouth, Bailey regretted it. Frustration had been forming all around her since she'd left Mom's house. Bailey knew she would have fun at the beach and being with Dad, but the first few days away from her routine with Mom seemed tough. Her surfing camp would start soon, and Crimson Island had a lot of history she wanted to explore. Most folks who lived here just called it the Island.

"We could make a list of fun things you want to do this summer." Dad was trying his best to cheer her up. "How about we start with airing up the tires on your bikes? You and Ben can see what's going on in the harbor this morning. I'll join you later for some jet-skiing."

Ben and Bailey rode their bikes through the quaint town that was a beautiful island. Dad's house was closer to the long beach that opened up to the ocean and had bigger waves. It was where they could surf.

The bay side of the island was a harbor where cruise ships came into port, and ships like the big banana boat docked to unload its yummy cargo. Yachts, sailboats, and speedboats all used the harbor when going out to sea.

White Ferry Landing was where the ferry dropped off passengers that came across the harbor from the mainland or took folks back from the island.

As they rode past the tourist shops and fresh market, Ben wanted to stop for ice cream, but he had forgotten to bring money. They came to the small beach near the harbor and sat in a grassy area to watch the water traffic. A few fishing boats were leaving, and a few people were getting their kayaks ready.

Several sandpipers came up from the water looking for a snack. Bailey wished she had something to feed the birds.

When their dad showed up with the jet ski, they jumped up and ran toward the dock. The only problem was that the twins had to take turns going with Dad.

Ben went first. He loved going fast and feeling the wind on his face. As the jet ski bounced over the wake made by other boats, Ben laughed. *This was great.* He begged Dad to let him drive, but Dad wouldn't go against the rules.

Bailey waited for her turn. She fastened her life vest and climbed on behind Dad. She put her arms around his waist and held on tight. Last summer they had a blast doing this. She was happy to be back on the jet ski with Dad.

But when Dad took off, and they hit some rough water, the bumps made Bailey's heart race. Fear clawed at her emotions, and she could hardly breathe. She began to panic and yelled at Dad to stop. *What is wrong with me?*

Dad immediately slowed down, turned the jet ski around and headed back to the landing. Bailey felt embarrassed, but she wanted to get off and out of the water. Dad tried to find out what was wrong. "I thought you loved this," he said.

Bailey felt ashamed. She didn't know why the ride scared her, but she was done and just wanted to go home.

Ben and Dad weren't done. And they didn't want to take her home. Dad couldn't leave the jet ski, and Bailey didn't want to wait on them. She was wet and cold and felt like a coward. *What is my problem?* She was confused and upset. She ran from the sandy shore toward the grassy area and flopped down.

As she looked toward the dock, she noticed Pops walking her way with his bike. It looked like he had just gotten off of the ferry that had come across the bay. He smiled and waved. *He remembers me!*

Pops introduced himself to Bailey, and she nodded. He asked her if she was okay. Bailey didn't know what to say.

She wasn't okay, but she didn't want to admit it. A big Evil Scoundrel of Embarrassment sat on her head. Another Scoundrel of Dejection poked her thoughts.

Pops noticed she was shaking and in wet swimwear and asked if she had been swimming. Bailey shook her head. "My dad and brother are on the jet ski. I got scared and wanted off." *Why did you tell him that?*

Pops parked his bicycle and sat down in the grass next to her. "I'm sorry," he said, gently. Pops didn't know what words would ease the pain this little girl was feeling, but he did know what he could do.

Silently, he began to pray for God to send His comfort to her hurting emotions. In answer to his prayers, God sent angels to bring peace and His Holy Spirit to whisper encouragement in her heart.

Bailey felt happy that Pops had cared enough to just sit with her. He didn't try to make her explain why she was scared or use a lot of words to make her feel better. She didn't know he had prayed, and she didn't see the response of heaven, but she felt lighter and hopeful.

They watched the ships entering the harbor. Several sailors waved at the folks watching from the shoreline.

Pops' cell phone rang. It was Grins checking on him. He explained that he was on his way home but had seen Bailey at White Ferry Landing and was spending time with her.

Bailey couldn't hear what Grins was saying, but Pops laughed and assured her that he hadn't stopped for a cupcake.

They looked towards the water and saw Dad and Ben slowly bring the jet ski close to shore. Pops waved and pointed at Bailey and then at himself. He made hand motions to let Todd, her dad, know he would take Bailey back home.

Todd nodded his agreement and signaled the okay with a thumbs-up. Crimson Island was like a small town, and most everyone was helpful and caring. Most folks had lived here a long time and knew each other.

Pops raised his bike's kickstand. "Did you ride your bike to the Landing?" He looked around.

Bailey nodded toward the bike rack near the beach and began walking to it.

As they rode back together, Pops pedaled slower as they went past the park. He explained that there were over fifty different kinds of trees in it. Bailey could see a playground at one end.

He told her stories about his life on the Island as a young boy. He'd loved the ocean, surfing, fishing, and sailing.

Pops showed her the road that would take them to Point Crim Lighthouse. Bailey hoped to go there sometime. She could tell he loved this place.

Bailey thought the stories and history were fascinating. She wanted to tell Dad and Ben all about it. Then she remembered how she had run off from them. They would probably be upset with her. She sighed. She just wanted to have a fun summer, and so far, it wasn't. She missed Mom. She wondered if Mom was lonely without them. She would call her soon.

Grins was waiting at the house when they walked up. "There you two are," she said, grinning. "I hope you're hungry. I've got sandwiches and fruit ready. And I have two good surprises!"

Chapter 2

Bailey was ready for good things. Grins was grinning. "Our grandson arrives later this evening. And I was able to get reservations for the Grunion Run tomorrow night."

Bailey had no idea what the Grunion Run was, and Grins explained. "There's a beach up the coast that has a species of slender, silvery fish called grunion. They swim in from the ocean at night to spawn in the sand of the beach. During full moon with a high tide, you can dig in the sand and catch them with your hands."

Pops chuckled. "This is your kind of fishing, isn't it?" He was teasing her.

"I guess it is," she laughed. "I've always wanted to take Andy, that's our grandson, and this time it's working out. I hope your dad says yes." She looked at Bailey. "We can all go together."

They ate lunch on the front porch and watched as beach-goers walked toward the beach with their towels and picnic baskets. Bailey asked Grins if she would go with her to collect some shells. Grins reminded her that early morning was the best time to find seashells, but she agreed to walk along the shoreline anyway.

Grins was right. There weren't many shells on the beach in the afternoon, but the warm sand in her toes made Bailey feel happy. They strolled near the water's edge, letting the waves ripple over their feet.

There were kids with sand buckets building castles. Several people were throwing a frisbee back and forth. Umbrellas were everywhere, and picnics were spread out on towels. They stopped to watch the ships that looked tiny because they were far out in the ocean.

When they got back, Dad and Ben were sitting on the front porch with Pops. Bailey waved, and Dad looked relieved that she was okay. Ben ran to greet her. "We're going to the Grunion Run!"

He was excited. He had heard about it, but never had the chance to go before.

That afternoon, Andy arrived with his parents. Grins hugged them all. She was excited to be spending time with Andy again. "You've grown so tall since I've seen you," Grins said, admiring him from head to toe.

Andy laughed. "I'm happy to see you, too." He was eager to spend time at the beach and was happy to be with his grandparents. This summer would probably be less hard work than the one he'd spent at the farm.

Andy brought in his suitcase and Grins told him all about the fun things she and Pops had planned for their time together. "There's even a boy your age next door," she said as he was putting his things in the closet.

Andy whipped around. "Wow! Just wow!" he exclaimed. *That was great news!* He loved being with Grins and Pops but having someone his age would be even more fun at the beach. Andy silently thanked God for this surprise. He hoped this boy could surf.

Andy's parents were going up the coast for a conference and wanted to continue on their trip. Pops persuaded them to take time to eat together first, and they all walked to a burger joint a few blocks away. After a quick meal, Andy hugged his parents' good-bye and asked Grins if they could go to the beach and at least get his feet wet.

Pops and Grins both wanted to go, and the three of them headed towards the ocean. When Andy got to the sandy beach, he pulled off his shoes and ran barefoot through the squishy sand to the water. *Brr, it was cold!* He'd forgotten that part about the Pacific Ocean.

Pops pointed toward some big rocks near the Crimson Island Hotel. "Let's see if we can find some crabs in those rocks." Looking closer, part of the rock looked like it moved. Those were crabs in their crevices. Andy picked one up and examined it. Crabs always seemed like they were crawling sideways.

He put it back carefully and saw some tiny fish swimming in the tidepools. He loved the beach and the sea life of the ocean.

Andy could hardly wait to get into the water, but the sun was beginning to set, and the three of them decided to walk back to the house.

Andy knew he was too excited in his new surroundings to be able to sleep and Pops asked if he wanted to walk to White Ferry Landing and have a late-night snack. Grins just shook her head but grinned at them. "At least we'll be getting our exercise," Pops told her, laughing. He did have a sweet tooth.

As the two of them walked through the streets of the charming island town, the angels that had always been with them, were there, too. Bak and Dels were watchful of Andy. They knew that as always, God had great things in store for him and they were happy to be on assignment.

Pops was gone when Andy woke up the next morning. He was serving as a tour guide at the Point Crim Lighthouse Museum.

After breakfast, Grins asked Andy to join her as she read her Bible. They read the story of the Good Shepherd from John, chapter 10.

Andy remembered his teacher at church telling the kids how important it was to hear God's voice. He knew about sheep from visiting his cousins' farm. Sheep follow their shepherd's voice because they know he takes care of them and they can trust him.

Andy wanted to bring God's goodness to others. He was learning to recognize God's gentle voice inside of him. Andy felt light as they finished their special time with God. Although the human beings didn't see them, angels had joined in their time of worship to God.

When they heard a noise outside, Andy ran to the front window and saw a boy and girl his age. They were shouting at each other.

"Is that the boy next door that you told me about?" Andy asked. "And who is the girl?"

Grins nodded. "That's Ben and his twin sister, Bailey. I wonder what's going on." Andy wasn't sure he wanted to meet them in the middle of an argument, but Grins needed to give Bailey a book that would help her identify shells.

Andy followed Grins down the sidewalk. The twins stopped their shouting and looked embarrassed. Grins introduced Andy to them and gave Bailey the book.

Bailey thanked her and explained that they had a big chore to do. "Dad asked us to clean out the garage. It's quite a mess."

"It's not even our stuff," Ben said, annoyed. "Dad came to live here, and our grandparents left this stuff behind." He pointed to the open garage. They could see boogie boards, life vests, a canoe, fishing gear and nets strewn everywhere.

"That is a lot of stuff," Andy said, looking at the variety of things that were hanging on the walls and lying on the floor. He walked toward the boogie boards.

"I'd rather be surfing," Ben scowled.

"The fog hasn't cleared yet," Bailey reminded him. "Dad asked us to do this project first today."

"Like I said, this stuff isn't my problem. I shouldn't have to help clean it up." Ben didn't see the Evil Scoundrel of Frustration that wanted him to feel worse.

Bailey folded her arms and huffed as she sat on an old box. Ben gave her an angry look. "We'll never get anything done if you just sit." His words were not kind.

They began to argue again. The Scoundrel of Criticism was slithering next to Bailey. Another Scoundrel of Insecurity was trying to punch her emotions. "I hear she has a great destiny, and I've been sent to make sure she doesn't find out the truth, or we're doomed," the first Scoundrel snarled.

Andy just wanted to get out of there and play his new video game. Grins thought it seemed like the fog outside had rolled inside to their attitudes.

Just then, Todd, the twins' dad opened the door from the house. "Wow!" He looked surprised when he saw all of them together. He waved at Grins and nodded at Andy as she introduced him.

Ben kicked a rusty bucket, and it clattered into some fishing gear and made it fall with a crash. Bailey held her hands over her ears and squealed. Andy hopped away as some white and

20

red bobbers started rolling on the floor. He stumbled over a mesh net. It was a tangled mess.

"Look," Dad said to the twins. "I told you to clean this up so we know what we have and what new things we should get. Please get to work!" He sounded upset. "There's a big trash can for what's broken or torn, and the things that need repair can be put on this workbench." Dad closed the door and went back inside the house.

The kids were tense and grumpy. Ben began throwing things into the trash can as hard as he could. Bailey glared at him. "Those aren't all broken, Ben! You should be careful."

As Ben picked up an old oar from underneath the upside-down canoe, something scurried out from under it. He jumped back.

Bailey saw it and shrieked! "What is that?" Andy hopped out of the way and knocked over an old paint can as a gray, furry shape with a long tail scampered over the trash and around the corner of the garage.

Grins grabbed a broom and began to chase it. "That looked like a rat!" she shouted as she took off behind it. But the rat was fast and already gone.

The inside door flew open. Todd poked his head out. "What is all the noise about?" He wasn't happy. "I'm trying to get some work done for my job on the computer in here, and all I hear is a bunch of rattling. Can't you pick things up more quietly?" His voice got louder and louder. He looked at Grins with the broom in her hand. "What..." he didn't finish his sentence before Ben began to yell.

"This garage is a disaster, Dad. And now we have rats! I'm done!" He stomped off.

"It's true, Dad." Bailey began whining. "We just saw a rat come out from under the old canoe and run around the corner. What if there's more?"

The Evil Scoundrels started to jump around in a frenzy. They loved anger and selfishness. They knew those emotions could destroy people and they liked to see children growing up with angry attitudes and bad behavior that would continue throughout their lives. Their every intention was to stir up trouble.

Dad rubbed both of his hands over his face and sighed. Impatience poked at his thoughts. He didn't know what to do. He slammed the door and went back inside.

Grins took her phone out of her pocket and turned on some praise music. She prayed and asked God for His peace to come to them.

Angels came in response to the prayers and praise to God. The peace and joy they brought began to touch each heart in the garage.

Grins spoke quietly with a gentle voice. "You all have a choice," she said. "God loves you. He has good plans for your life, but you have an enemy who wants evil for you."

The twins didn't know what enemy Grins was talking about. She continued, "Our enemy is Satan, and he wants to destroy us. He uses Evil Scoundrels from his dark realm to try to trick us into making bad choices."

She told the kids that the Bible says the fruit of God's Spirit is love. Love shows up in joy and kindness. When we are patient and kind to others, those things come from God."

The kids began listening quietly as the music played in the background. Their choices had made them more miserable. Bailey had started to sniffle. A tear ran down her cheek. Ben stared at the floor and looked glum.

Grins wasn't done. She knew this was a moment God could use for learning something good when it looked like something bad. "We're not robots. God created human beings to have free will and follow His ways because they choose to. When we choose selfishness and hatred, angry yelling or anything evil, we partner with Evil Scoundrels instead of God's goodness." They listened as she told them how much their choices matter.

Bailey wiped her tears. Ben looked around the garage and shook his head.

Andy was thinking about the Bible story they read that morning. Jesus had said He came to give life that was full and good. They had also learned that the thief comes to steal and destroy.

He was having a hard time not feeling sorry for himself. He wanted to be in the ocean or riding his skateboard.

Andy recognized a voice inside of him and began to think about a solution. "I could help you," he blurted out. *Did I really say that? Do I mean it?* He looked around at the piles of stuff that needed to be cleaned up and organized.

"That's a great idea," he heard Grins say. "We could make it fun." The twins looked at her like she was silly.

"I have an idea," Andy said looking around and pointing. "Trash pile, good stuff pile, 'I'm not sure' pile. And," he laughed, "How about a garage sale pile?"

Grins clapped and turned up the music. She began to dance around the room. She looked funny, and they all laughed. The heavenly beings pushed out the Evil Scoundrels as praise to God brought kindness.

Bailey began smiling as she sorted through the fishing lures. Ben started to pick up the canoe and Andy helped him turn it over. Grins began sorting through the old cans of paint and silently thanked God for bringing peace.

Everyone was sorting and cleaning, and soon the various piles began to look organized. Working together made the garage cleanup much quicker and easier. They stayed alert for more rats.

The garage suddenly seemed brighter. Bailey looked toward the beach. "The fog has lifted," she shouted as she did a little dance. Sure enough, the sun was peeking through the clouds.

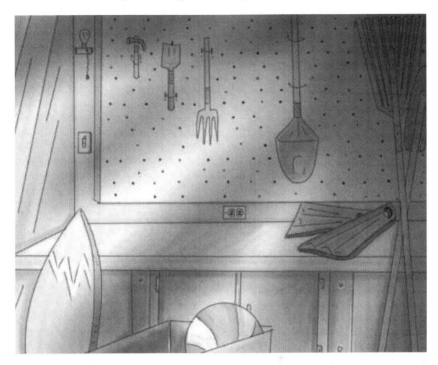

When Dad opened the door again, he raised his eyebrows. "This looks great!" He was impressed with their hard work.

"We certainly know there's only one good boogie board here," Ben said. He pointed to the trash pile. "Those wouldn't be safe in the ocean anymore."

"That's your pile, Dad," Bailey said. "It's the 'I don't know' one!"

Her dad laughed. "I can take care of that one." He patted Grins on the shoulder. "I'll help my kids finish up here. Thanks to you and Andy for your help. It looks a lot better and helps me know what is still usable and what needs to be replaced. I'll need to get some new things."

The kids made plans to meet at the beach. Grins said she would pack a picnic lunch while Ben and Bailey finished the garage and got into their suits.

Andy wanted to play his new video game when they got back to Grins' house but decided to ask how he could help with packing their lunch. "I'm good at fixing lunches," he laughed. "We did this together on the farm."

Grins nodded. "We sure did! You were a great help that summer on the farm."

At the beach, Bailey found a spot that was perfect for building sandcastles. She used a plastic shovel to help her create a design and a bucket with water to keep the sand wet enough to shape into a castle. Ben and Andy helped her get started, then went swimming.

Bailey told Ben she didn't want to get cold in the water. When they started throwing a frisbee on the beach, she joined them. Todd walked up just as Ben's friends came by and asked him to surf. Ben told them he hadn't brought his surfboard but introduced them to his dad and

Andy. The boys made plans to meet and surf another day.

Grins was relaxing in her beach chair with her nose in a book. Andy walked over and told her he was starving. He got food from the basket and the others joined him. As they ate lunch together, Andy asked Ben about surfing.

"It's easier to show than tell," Ben said. Ben didn't want Andy to know about his bad experience and told him he was still learning.

"You could start with boogie boarding," Ben advised. "I can help you pick one out."

Andy looked at Grins. She nodded. "Good idea. When Pops gets back, he can give you some lessons."

Bailey wanted to stay on the beach and finish her sandcastle. Grins was happy to keep reading her book. Todd said he needed to get back to the house to do some work and gave the boys directions to the nearest store that had boogie boards. Andy wanted to get a wetsuit, too.

Andy got his wallet. The boys decided to go on their skateboards. Andy realized later that might not have been the best decision. Bringing the new boogie board back to the house was kind of tricky on a skateboard. Ben laughed at Andy as he tried to balance the load he was carrying while skateboarding.

Finally, Andy decided to walk and carry his stuff. Ben was circling him and did a few kickflips. Andy knew he was showing off, but he just kept telling Ben how good he was doing. He didn't want to get frustrated and lose the peace that was so important to him.

The boys got back with Andy's new boogie board just as Pops drove up in his old car. He didn't usually drive the 1968 red Mustang convertible around the island except for shows or in parades. He'd had it for a long time, and he took good care of it. Andy hoped to ride with him in the parade that was coming soon.

Andy showed Pops the new boogie board and told him they were going back to the beach. Pops offered to go with them and give Andy some lessons.

Pops told him to look where a bulge formed at the highest peak of the wave, pointing the nose of the board toward the beach.

"If you paddle and kick, then put yourself in the belly of the wave, you'll be able to glide right on to the beach." Andy tried hard.

"It's important to be equally balanced on the board," Pops called out to him. "Remember to match the speed of the wave and the wave will pick you up and do the work."

Andy found smaller and less powerful waves to try. Ben showed him how to lean left to turn left and lean right to turn right. He kept trying over and over. His awkward tries made him laugh.

He had to spit out the salty water that went up his nose. Andy thought he was getting better as he kept trying. Ben stayed next to him and helped as he learned.

They were having a great time. This was going to be even better than he'd imagined. Pops told them he would take them jet-skiing soon if they wanted to. *If they wanted to? Of course, they wanted to.* Andy was hoping he could try surfing soon, too.

Chapter 3

Everyone had made plans to meet in time to drive up the coast together for the Grunion Run. It was after dark when they reached the entrance for the event. All three kids were excited about this adventure. None of the adults or kids had been here before.

As they parked and went toward the observation area, they gave the tickets and got their hands stamped.

Together they walked down a long ramp that led to the shoreline. They each had a flashlight. Ben ran ahead and saw them first. "There's tons of fish flopping on the sand," he shouted to the others.

Their little group hurried to where he was standing on the beach. Waves were rolling in around their feet and washing the fish onto the sand.

It was the highest tide of the month. The time was right for these fish to mate. The eggs laid in the sand would hatch in about ten days.

As hundreds of fish were wiggling on the sand, they could grab them in their hands. Bailey and Andy caught several and tossed them into the bucket. Ben had a big handful.

With their admission ticket, they were allowed to catch one bucketful. Pops wanted to cook them. Even Grins was touching the slithering silver and white fish.

The water was so cold; Ben felt as though he'd stuck his hands in a glass of ice water. With each fresh wave, more fish would come wiggling in, and others would be washed back out to sea.

"This is amazing!" Todd looked at Pops. "I've never seen so many fish in one place."

Pops nodded. "It sure beats waiting for a long time with a fishing pole on shore."

Two weeks previously the tide had been high, and the eggs were buried in the sand. Seeing the newly hatched fish squiggling in the sandy beach was exciting.

As they went back to the indoor hatchery area, the guide gave each of them an empty baby food jar. She had a mixture of sand and water that had been kept for two weeks and was now emptied into their jars. All they had to do was swirl the sand and water around for sixty seconds, and the fish would hatch.

They watched their jars in amazement. It was as if the eggs popped like popcorn, exploding into tiny fish. "Look at them!" Pops was excited and showed Andy his jar. Several baby fish were starting to swim around.

"Wow! Just wow!" Andy exclaimed. "How does this happen?" he asked the guide.

"Each female lays around 2,000 eggs. After being fertilized, the glob of eggs stays moist deep in the sand although the top is dry. The conditions of the water and incoming surf at high tide causes them to hatch."

The guide shook the jar gently. "Shaking this jar is similar to what the waves of the surf are like, and fish develop. Sand can be collected and put in buckets for ten days."

Grins was having fun gently shaking her jar. Bailey was delighted. They all followed the guide back to the water's edge and gently emptied the tiny hatched fish into the ocean. "That is an awesome design of our great Creator-God." Grins laughed. "God is very creative. How wonderful to see these fish hatch!"

Mera, a worshipping angel, soared over them with ribbons of beautiful light reflecting off the water. Other angels joined this moment with their heavenly music as the earthly beings lifted thankful hearts towards heaven for God's amazing creation.

It was a fun trip and very late when they arrived home. No one had wanted to leave the grunion fish on the beach. They decided to only keep enough for one meal since Pops told them they would have to clean their own.

When they got back to the Island, the kids went straight to bed. Pops brought his fish in to clean them and prepare them for frying later.

The next morning was rainy, and Ben was sick. He hadn't slept well. His throat hurt, and he was coughing a lot. Bailey had left early for Surf Camp, and he was feeling lonely.

Dad was trying to work in his home office, but he couldn't focus, and he didn't seem very happy about it. The Scoundrels from the evil realm were having a hey-day with the sickness and tiredness in this household.

Discouragement bounced all around Dad's head. All he could think about was the time and money he was losing by not working and having to care for his sick son. Anger slammed into his thoughts, and he began to pace back and forth in the front room.

Gere and Fortif were Dad's angels and they knew there was an unseen battle that was going on in this house. They also knew God would bring His goodness.

Dad's cell phone rang. Grins was calling to check on them. Ben had been coughing a lot on the way home last night, and she was concerned.

Dad tried to be calm as he told her he couldn't get any work done with Ben being sick. Grins thought he sounded discouraged and a bit angry about the situation. She listened calmly and began to pray silently for God's wisdom. She could hear Ben coughing in the background.

"May Andy and I come over and pray for Ben?" she asked. Dad wasn't sure it was a good idea

since he didn't want them to get the germs from their house and get sick, too. But the thought of prayer did make him feel better.

His angels began to dance around him. They knew things would change when prayer to God began.

Grins soon rang the doorbell. Andy went over to Ben, who was laying on the couch with his cough syrup and blanket close by. Grins sat down next to him and felt his forehead. "You seem to have a fever," she said.

Ben nodded and coughed. The Evil Scoundrels of Gloom and Despair clawed at Ben's thoughts. They were planning a party for the sickness. They wanted it to grow and become pneumonia.

They invited their gang of evil partners to join them. Strife arrived with his ugly eyes glowing. He taunted the other scoundrels. "You just couldn't do this without me, could you?" The Evil Scoundrels snarled at each other.

Grins asked Todd if he would join her and Andy in praying for Ben. The Evil Scoundrels let out a growl. They did not like what was happening. They knew prayer would knock them out and they would fail their destructive mission.

Andy sat on the couch and prayed for his new friend. He asked God to come into the room and bring His goodness. Grins began to sing. When the words, 'God is so good' came out of her mouth, things changed quickly. The room filled with heavenly beings who joined her song.

The Evil Scoundrels began to shake when God's goodness was recognized. Grins angels, Kerte and Mijo, who went everywhere with her, stared with a blazing power at Despair. Gloom tried to hiss but was shriveling. The angels took their flaming swords and slashed through the ugly mass of awful scoundrels. The bad-smelling Despair was defeated.

The heavenly beings of love and goodness began to spin with divine light and all of the Evil Scoundrels became jittery, knowing they were failing. Discouragement and Strife tried to hang on and wrestle with the heavenly beings of God's goodness that flowed into the room as Grins kept singing.

But they were no match for the power that came with praise to God, and they limped away, squashed by the greatness of the heavenly beings brought by the prayers and praise to God.

Ben was still coughing. Andy knelt down and put his hand on Ben's arm. Grins put her hands next to Andy's. All the angels joined their prayer of faith for healing, and Ben stopped coughing. He began to breathe deeply.

Dad looked surprised. Ben's angels, Yilt and Lontoo, did high fives. More heavenly messengers filled the room with hope, creating rainbow light and glory clouds in the invisible realm.

Ben sat up. His angels were right there with him. He couldn't see them as they brushed his cheeks with their wings but he felt something like a fresh sea breeze wash over his whole body.

Grins put her hand on his forehead. It was still warm. She closed her eyes again. She spoke a verse from the Bible as a prayer to God. Her angels danced and worshipped Jesus. Surges of light entered the room as the glory of heaven touched earth.

When Grins thanked Jesus in her prayer for what He had done on the cross, the room erupted with joy from heaven. The heavenly beings sang and danced and spun light beams like lasers. The angels raised their swords in holy worship to Jesus. And the leftover pieces of Evil Scoundrels and sickness vanished. They could not stay where there was thankfulness for Jesus' love.

Although the human beings didn't see the frenzy of activity, their earthly senses could tell something had happened. Dad smelled a fragrance in the air that was like lilacs blooming. Peace had replaced all the Evil Scoundrels.

Dad hugged Ben and then sat back in amazement. "Your forehead isn't hot anymore," he said. Ben jumped up and spun around. He grinned at Andy and used his favorite words. "Wow! Just wow!"

Andy was pumping his fist. It was exciting when God's power was displayed and he got to be a part of it. Todd looked at Grins and Andy. "Thank you," he said, beaming.

Grins raised her hands to the heavens. "Thank You, Jesus!" she said. Andy was clapping like he did when someone scored a touchdown in a football game. He was so happy his friend was no longer sick. He was double happy since he really wanted to spend time that day in the ocean with Ben.

Ben, his dad, and Grins did a group hug. The angels did a group sword raising, then swooped through the cloud of glory and the fragrance of joy that filled the room.

Ben could hardly believe it. He knew his fever had been real and he knew it was gone now. He wanted to ask Andy how they had done it, but he wasn't sure what to ask. Ben was just happy he was better and realized he was hungry.

"Can we fix something to eat, Dad?" Ben asked. Dad laughed and nodded. Andy looked at Grins and asked if they could stay. Grins grinned. "This room is so full of joy right now; I want to stay here and enjoy it."

Todd looked at Grins. "You've got to teach me how this prayer stuff works," he said. "That was amazing!"

Grins nodded. "I'll be happy to tell you more anytime."

Just then Pops knocked on the door. Andy raced to open it and nearly ran into him. "Oops, sorry Pops," Andy said.

"You almost got grunion all over you, young man!" Pops was trying not to slosh any of the water out and hurried toward the kitchen sink.

Todd helped him with the fish as they put them in plastic bags. Todd had offered to grill them and make fish tacos that evening if Pops did the cleaning. Pops thought it was a good trade-off. They were hard to cook.

The boys decided to eat a quick bowl of cereal so they could get to the ocean. Laughter filled the kitchen.

Pops noticed how happy everyone seemed and was thankful, remembering the night before had been cold and late.

The heavenly beings were still dancing in dazzling light. They loved doing their part in bringing heaven's goodness to earth. They knew God had great things for Ben's life, and they knew Bailey was getting to know God at camp, too.

Chapter 4

Bailey had been so excited about going to Surf Camp this year. She had never been away from her family alone at night. Her brother, Ben, was a pretty good surfer and she wanted to be good at it, too. Mom had suggested this camp and Bailey agreed to go.

Although she never told anyone, Bailey was afraid of the ocean. She had been pulled under a wave by a rip current last year, and although her dad pulled her out quickly, she had been terrified.

Her angels, Jeray and Bistoe, had been right there, watching over her in that dangerous moment. Jeray was the one who had lifted her out of the water so her dad could see where she was and rescue her. But Bailey never saw the angels.

Now she was doubly afraid. Camp had seemed like a good idea to learn the skills she wanted for becoming a surfer, but she knew she would have to face being in the ocean as she learned. It was also very hard not to have Mom or Dad with her at night when she went to bed.

The Evil Scoundrels of Fear and Anxiety began to torment Bailey's thoughts. She was shaking as she stepped into the ocean the first day. Her camp leader, Sara, thought she must be cold. Sara asked her if she needed more than her wetsuit to keep her warm. Bailey couldn't even reply to Sara because she was starting to cry.

Sara prayed for wisdom to help Bailey. She knelt next to Bailey and wrapped her arms around her. Bailey sobbed into Sara's shoulder as Sara gently rubbed her back. Jeray and Bistoe wielded their swords against the Evil Scoundrel of Fear that was tormenting Bailey.

Sara took Bailey's hands into hers and looked into her troubled eyes. "Did something happen to you in the water when you were younger?" she asked. Bailey nodded with tears streaming down her face. "Tell me about it," Sara spoke kindly.

They sat down in the sand and Bailey told her the story. It had been a memory that brought fear when she stepped into the ocean. Sara asked her if they could pray about it together. Bailey nodded. "Let's ask God to show you that He was always with you, even in those moments when you felt alone and afraid."

As Sara prayed, Bailey remembered the ocean wave that pulled her underwater. She suddenly saw something bringing her out of the wave to sit on top of it. It was a glowing white flash of light that held her up until her dad turned in her direction and saw her.

Jeray did a summersault flip over their heads. It had been a moment of assignment by God. Bailey turned to Sara. "I think God sent an angel to show my dad where I was so he could rescue me. I just saw a memory of a part I've never seen before." She told Sara about the brilliant light that seemed to lift her above the water.

Sara raised her hand and thanked God. "Yes! That's so good!" She hugged Bailey and told her how much God loved her. Sara and Bailey's angels were raising their swords and taking out the Evil Scoundrels that had been destructive, slicing through their grip on Bailey's memories.

They didn't want to let go of her, but the truth that God was always taking care of her, had brought freedom to Bailey's mind. No fear or anxiety could stay where truth lived.

"When you get to your room, read Psalm 91 in your Bible," Sara said. "There's a verse that says God gives His angels charge over us. I believe that's what happened to you then, and those angels are still there to care for you now." Jeray and Bistoe took a bow, acknowledging their position and showing gratitude to God who is all-knowing.

Sara's angels danced with pleasure and glory around the beach, joining Jeray and Bistoe. Bailey felt free and happy as she began her lessons. She felt so peaceful in the water, and the other kids were amazed at how quickly she found her balance point on her surfboard.

Sara taught her group that rip currents are a surfer's best friend but can cause a swimmer to panic. "You want to get pulled out into the waves as a surfer, but as a swimmer, they can pull you under the water."

Bailey knew that the outgoing tide was when more water was pulled back from the beach and created bigger waves. Tides were important to understand for safety with ocean sports. She felt so free now that her fear was completely gone. Bailey was still careful and followed Sara's instructions.

When class time ended, her body was tired, but her emotions were light, and she felt confident. She couldn't wait to tell her brother, Ben, how much fun she was having as she learned to surf. He had always wanted her to go with him and now she knew she could.

She made new friends and they asked how she had learned so fast. Bailey wasn't sure what to tell them. Sara sat down with them for lunch and encouraged Bailey to tell them her story. The girls cheered as she told them about the God-moment she had experienced.

Another girl told them how God had healed her body when she was stung by a bee. Several others had stories of God-moments, too. Bailey was happy to hear so many wonderful stories.

As she returned to her bunk at the camp, she remembered to look up the Bible verses that Sara had given her. Verse 2 was about trusting God because He is the place of safety. When she came to verse 5, she read it over and over. It said not to be afraid of the terrors of the night.

That was another hard place for Bailey. She stopped reading and wondered what caused her to be afraid at night. She didn't remember anything scary that had happened; she just knew that darkness and night time had always brought fear to her heart.

She kept reading the rest of Psalm 91. There was the verse about the angels protecting her wherever she went. She read about God rescuing and protecting those who trust in His name. Bailey had heard about Jesus, and she loved God, but she wanted to know Him personally as a best friend.

She wasn't sure what to say or do or how to pray, so she lifted her hands toward heaven as Sara had done and just said, "Thank you."

Her angels began to worship God. Heavenly Beings of Love and Peace zoomed into the room and joined in the celebration of what was to come. The Evil Scoundrels who hated everything good, kicked and scratched at the torture that God's light brought to their plan for evil.

God had great plans for Bailey, and the Enemy Scoundrels were fighting against His good plan. They were losing because Bailey was choosing to believe His Word, the Bible.

Bailey's days at Camp were filled with learning surfing skills, new friends, and sand volleyball. Her roommates prayed every night, and she didn't even think about her fear of the dark.

She called Mom and thanked her for picking this camp for her. Mom wanted to hear all about it. Bailey told her mom the good stories of God's love that the campers had shared.

She could tell Mom was crying and her voice got shaky when she told about the angel rescuing her with Dad, and her nighttime fear being gone. She asked Mom if she was lonely without her and Ben.

"Of course, I miss you both terribly," she said. "But hearing your stories and the good things you are experiencing makes it worth it."

Bailey and her friends took a break from surfing one afternoon to have a sand castle competition.

Each team carefully crafted a large castle using buckets to shape the roof. They forgot the tide would be coming in and a wave made their castle look like it had melted into a mess. They'd also forgotten an important rule of the beach. Never turn your back to the ocean.

"It looks like the ocean won," Bailey laughed, looking at what was left of her castle.

"We're already a sandy mess," one of the girls said with a grin. "Maybe we should make sand angels like we do in the snow." She didn't have to say it again. The kids flopped onto the sand and flapped their arms and legs. Their bodies were now covered in sand, so they ran to the ocean to wash off.

The last morning after breakfast there was class time with a special speaker. The speaker was a famous surfer named Jackson Cole. Bailey couldn't wait to tell Ben about him.

Jackson was going to show them some of his skills in the ocean, but he told them about his life first. He told the campers about a car accident that nearly killed him. He had chosen to believe there was no God until the moment he thought he would die. He had cried out for God to save him and he had survived and gotten a second chance.

He told the surfers that when he opened his heart to God, it was as though heaven opened up and goodness began to flow from God into his heart. Jackson described his friendship with God and told the kids it was what God wanted for each of them.

"God is like having the kindest father who only wants good for you." He described knowing God to be the best thing ever. "The way to God is through His Son, Jesus. Asking Him to be in charge of your life gives you a great exchange. He takes your sin and gives you His gift of eternal life."

The whole room was quiet. "God gives every person free will. You can choose whether you want Him in your life or not. Jesus dying for your sins on the cross was real. He made it simple for you. He did the hard part. He was the sacrifice."

Jackson went to the whiteboard and wrote A, B and C. He looked at the kids. "A is that you admit you have sinned and need Him in your life. B is that you believe Jesus is the only way to have eternal life and C is that you commit your life to Him as your Savior and Lord.

Bailey smiled. She was ready to do this. She believed Jesus was the only Son of God and the only way to eternal life. She wanted Him to live in her heart, and she wanted to live to please Him.

When Jackson led them in a prayer, she prayed aloud. She felt as though a warm liquid was being poured through her whole body. Lightness and brightness filled her.

Jeray and Bistoe were bouncing in brilliant glitter and flashes of rainbow light. They soared through the walls and ceiling with excitement and great joy. Heaven's host had come to join the celebration of humans giving their hearts to follow Jesus.

The few leftover Evil Scoundrels of Unbelief vaporized as the room filled with angels dancing and worshipping the God of the universe. It was as though sparkles of gold dust floated through the air and landed on each of the kids.

The joy that filled Bailey's heart caused her to raise her arms as high as she could to worship and thank Jesus. Bailey knew this was a moment that would change her life forever. She couldn't wait to tell Ben all that had happened to her.

After their prayer time, the group walked with Jackson to the beach. They watched in awe as the famous surfer did cutbacks and aerial flips. He made it look easy to fly over the waves in the shape of an S.

It made Bailey's heart pound. She cheered with the others and couldn't wait to try some of those tricks as she improved her skills.

The heavenly beings were still dancing in radiant light and doing their own aerial flips. The best adventures on earth were children choosing to follow God and letting Him be in charge of their lives.

After her wonderful time at Surf Camp, Bailey was excited to tell Ben about her experiences. She got home after Ben was sleeping. The Evil Scoundrels were not happy about the way things were going, and they began to pull in some helpers to blast at Bailey's joy.

Sickness attacked first with some germs that had been picked up at camp. Bailey hadn't remembered to use proper handwashing, and she felt as though she was coming down with a cold.

The Evil Scoundrel of Misery whimpered around her as she woke up in her bed back at Dad's house. It was a cloudy and gray day outside. Gloom snuck into the room and began to peck at Bailey's thoughts. Another Scoundrel of Dejection jumped on top of her and tried to dump a load of negative thoughts into her mind. She felt sad.

Bailey's angels were busy, too. They brought her good memories of what Jesus had done in saving her life, not only from the near-drowning but the sweet love of knowing she belonged to Jesus.

She sat up in bed and began coughing. Dad heard her and walked into her room to check on her. She smiled and hugged him. She had missed him while she was at camp.

Heavenly beings danced with the love that was flowing in the room. They knew that hugs with parents and their children show the love of God the Father toward His earthly children.

Jeray and Bistoe did high fives. Peace entered the room and affection became a powerful force against the Enemy Scoundrels' efforts at putting confusion into Bailey's mind.

Courage rose up strong in Bailey's heart as she took her Dad's hand and looked into his eyes. "I want to tell you all about my experiences at camp," she said. "But first I'm going to take a shower and get dressed."

"I heard coughing and thought you sounded sick," Dad said.

Bailey thought about what she had learned. "I learned that I have an enemy who wants to destroy me, Dad. Sometimes sickness is used against me to try to affect my body, depress me or steal my joy. I'm going to fight against that with prayer while I take my shower. I think I will be fine."

Dad raised his eyebrows. He'd never heard Bailey talk like that, but he admired her attitude and nodded as he left the room.

Bailey began to sing the songs she'd learned at camp as she showered and got dressed. The coughing sometimes made her words sound funny, but she didn't stop. Jeray and Bistoe sang with her. The more she sang praises to God, the more heavenly beings filled the room. She remembered that worshipping God defeats any enemy.

Her enemies of Gloom and Dejection with their negativity began to slink away as joy and affection toward God and His goodness filled the room. The Evil Scoundrels that had threatened to take over Bailey's day covered their ears with the painful sounds of defeat that praising God brings to them.

They began to fight and taunt each other. "You're such a loser," Irritation said to Depression. Depression whipped his ugly black tail toward Irritation. "So, I'm a loser and I know it, but you were sent to help, and you stink at your job."

They kept snarling at each other as they slunk away from the room that had become filled with a holy Presence. God's glory was like an invisible cloud. "Sure don't want to be close to that!" Depression said. "So, we agree on one thing!" Irritation whimpered pitifully.

Bailey prayed for her body. She put her hand on her chest and thanked God that He was a good father and loved her and wanted the best for her. She remembered the Bible verse that says Jesus healed all the people's sicknesses and disease. She kept thanking God for His goodness; then she began to sing again. Heavenly beings danced for joy.

She opened her bedroom door and smelled bacon. Dad was cooking breakfast. Bailey rushed to him and gave him another hug.

"Wow!" he said, smiling. "You seem a whole lot better." At that moment the doorbell rang. She looked at her Dad, but he just shrugged and shook his head. He didn't know who it might be either.

Chapter 5

It was Grins. And she was grinning from ear to ear. "I've come to hear about your camp experiences," she said.

"You're just in time for breakfast," Dad said as he welcomed her.

"That's a bonus for me!" Grins said, laughing. "But where is Ben?"

"I was wondering about that, too," Bailey said, looking at Dad.

"He's been trying some golf lessons while you were gone and had to be at the course early. He'll be back in time for lunch," Dad assured her.

Bailey sighed. She didn't want to wait until Ben got back to tell them about Surf Camp. Grins and Dad listened carefully as she told about God healing her trauma of the near-drowning.

Dad had tears in his eyes and Grins clapped her hands with joy. "God is so good!" Grins said. "That's just wonderful."

"There's more," Bailey told them. "Jackson Cole was a speaker one morning, and he spoke about heaven and how we can know for certain that we will go there."

The heavenly beings filled the room with a dazzling light. They showed joy by jumping and bouncing up and down at the same time as only heavenly beings can do. This was one of their favorite subjects from human beings.

Grins stood up and did her own dance and twirl. Bailey laughed.

"You did it!" Grins said, delightedly. "You gave your heart to Jesus, didn't you?"

"Yes! Yes! Exactly!" Bailey responded and joined Grins in dancing and twirling around the kitchen. Bistoe and Jeray were ecstatic. The air in the room was like happy fireworks.

Dad was thankful that Bailey was so happy. His own heart began to open up as he remembered his experience with Jesus as a little boy.

His heart had said 'yes' to Jesus, but the Evil Scoundrel of Apathy had grown into a big giant in his life since then. He began to see clearly that his choices had not been toward Jesus but toward selfishness and pride.

An angel brought courage, and like a sword destroying evil, the lies that had become attitudes of apathy and self-reliance were cut away.

Dad was thinking back to college days when he wanted others to know how great he was. He had made some choices that took him away from hearing God's voice. Deep inside, he wanted to feel God's closeness again.

Bailey was teaching Grins one of the new songs she had learned as they cleaned up the kitchen after breakfast. They could sense the presence of God in the room.

Heavenly beings filled with goodness and joy lifted their songs of worship to God. These were holy moments. The air was filling with hope. There was warmth as the heavenly beings brought sweet memories of God's kindness to Dad's heart. Dad was silent.

Fortif, a powerful angel who had been with Dad since birth came with a sword of grace that fought against Pride and Regret. It became a battlefield as Dad's heart struggled with making a choice.

Tears had begun to roll down his cheeks. Bailey saw it and looked at Grins with a question in her eyes. She reached for Bailey's hand. "Let's pray for God's peace to come. This is a God-moment for your dad," she said quietly.

The heavenly beings were ecstatic because they could see God's love begin to soothe and heal hurtful wounds from his past. As Dad prayed silently, he chose to forgive the people who had failed him, rejected and hurt him. His tears became joy tears. He was grateful that God's Spirit had brought him to a place of forgiveness.

Dad stood up and looked at Bailey. "Your testimony from camp really touched my heart. I've asked God to forgive me for my apathy towards Him, and I want to turn to Him, not away from Him."

The angels could not contain their joy. There were high-fives all around as a heavenly host began praising God. It was a thrilling dance party. Bailey was so excited and used Andy's words. "Wow, Dad!" was all she could say. "Just wow!"

Grins began to dance and jump up and down. Dad and Bailey had to laugh at how funny it looked.

At that moment, the front door opened and Ben walked in with his golf clubs. He stopped and took in the scene of his dad's tear-streaked face, Bailey hugging him and Grins funny dance-jumping. He wasn't sure whether to laugh or be concerned. All he could say was, "What is going on here?"

Bailey ran to Ben and hugged him tightly. "Wow!" Ben said, "I kind of missed you, too."

Dad laughed through his tears. "Truth is, you really missed her!" Dad hugged Ben, too. Then Grins joined the hugging and Ben had to laugh.

All this hugging had made him forget about the bad morning he'd had at golf lessons. His angels, Yilt & Lontoo, danced a little jig. This genuine affection was what Ben needed.

The ugly and hurtful Evil Scoundrels of Embarrassment and Ridicule were being stomped on by the love of his family.

Bailey clapped her hands and began to tell Ben about her time at camp. He was amazed that she had gotten to hear Jackson Cole speak. "I remember reading about his accident and how he got religion after that," Ben said.

"It wasn't religion," Bailey said. "But, I know what you mean. That's what a lot of people call it, but it was knowing God like a friend, and I prayed for that, too."

Ben looked at her and wondered what she meant. "I'm not sure I understand," he said. "But you seem really happy and sort of light and well, I don't know how to explain it."

Bailey laughed. "That's exactly how I feel. You sure are good at words. I'm so glad you are my twin brother."

Yilt and Lontoo joined Jeray & Bistoe in a glorious dance. The heavenly beings knew that kind words were just what Ben needed at that moment when he had felt small and stupid at his golf lesson.

"I've got to get back to my house," Grins said. "Andy and Pops will be back soon. They went to try some fishing off the pier. They've been doing a lot of things while you were gone."

Todd walked with Grins to the door and stood outside to talk with her.

"I want to hear more about the camp," Ben said. "Did you learn some skills to help you with surfing? Are you still afraid of the deep water? Did you make new friends?"

Bailey laughed and told Ben she could only answer one question at a time. He nodded. "Maybe I could wait and tell you and Andy at the same time," Bailey said.

Suddenly an Evil Scoundrel of Jealousy saw an opportunity to attack Ben and make him feel bad. "Fine," he bellowed, louder than he had intended. "I guess I'm not that important to you!"

Bailey was stunned. What had just happened? She didn't mean to make her brother feel bad. It wasn't what she meant. He was making a big deal out of nothing. Her hurt feelings wanted to get back at him with a mean comment.

The Enemy Scoundrels tried to bring Insecurity to her and threatened to bump the peace out of her mind. But heavenly beings brought hope and patience to her as well. Bailey quickly chose patience and hope.

"I'm sorry I made you feel unimportant," she told Ben. "You are my twin and my best friend, and I never want to hurt you." Jeray & Bistoe were ecstatic. The honor and kindness Bailey had given to her brother would be enough to defeat the enemies of Jealousy and Insecurity. Ben smiled. He felt ashamed of his outburst.

"I want to hear about your golf lessons," Bailey said.

"There you go again!" Ben roared at her. "Digging into my business. I don't want to talk about golf lessons, and I'm pretty sure you don't really care about them." The Evil Scoundrels of Self-pity and Rejection began to jump around Ben's head. Ben felt dizzy. *What was wrong with him? Bailey didn't deserve his mean words.*

Bailey walked away from him and sat down at the kitchen table. Self-pity was attacking her, too. Jeray & Bistoe surrounded her and began to sing over her. She didn't hear it, but she felt it in her heart, and she made the choice to begin to sing.

As she sang, the words shifted her focus from herself to her amazing God. "He is wonderful, He is glorious, He takes all my fears away." The heavenly host joined in and began to fill the room until the Evil Scoundrels of Self-pity and Rejection had to slink away. They could not stay where there was such praise and love for Jesus.

Ben walked slowly toward the kitchen table and sat down next to Bailey. He couldn't look at her. Bailey quietly asked if he would tell her why golf had been so upsetting.

Ben waited a long time and finally shook his head. "I'm no good at golf, and the other guys laugh at me. I feel really stupid, and I want to quit."

Dad had entered the kitchen just in time to hear Ben's words, but Ben didn't see him. He stayed quiet for a moment and then remembered his decision to trust Jesus with everything in his life. That meant he could trust God for wisdom even in his parenting skills.

"I'm so sorry for your painful feelings," Bailey said kindly. "I felt that way a lot when I was learning to surf."

"I'm sorry, too," said Dad behind them. Ben jumped. He was embarrassed that Dad had heard what he said. "I know what that feels like, and I think I can help you if you let me."

Ben didn't know what to say. Scoundrels of Confusion and Shame were nipping at his thoughts. He hadn't wanted Dad to know how he felt. He was pretty sure Dad would just give him a lecture and make him feel more stupid.

Dad came over and put his hand on Ben's shoulder. "If you'll let me take you out to the golf course, I can give you some pointers. I was very clumsy when I first started. I'm sorry I haven't taken the time to teach you more. We can go out there this evening if you want?"

Ben was surprised. Dad had always been too busy with work and his own activities to take time for him. He only came to watch if there was a competition. But he would give him a chance and maybe it would help his golf skills. "Sure," he said. "If you have time."

Dad laughed softly. "I will make time because you are important to me, son. And I need to ask you to forgive me for not giving you my time so often when you needed me. I'm really sorry, and I've asked God to forgive me and help me be a better father. Can you forgive me, Ben?"

Dad's angels danced and cheered. Heavenly light flashed like lasers around the kitchen. God's glory shone all around as forgiveness flowed between father and son. Ben and Bailey's angels did flips and swirls as joy filled the room.

"Of course, Dad. Maybe I can get better," Ben said, as hope came to his heart.

That evening, father and son headed to the golf course. Dad encouraged Ben and gave him tips as they went from the driving range to the putting green.

His confidence grew as Dad showed him how to hold his driver and stand with his feet apart. On the way home, Ben was excited and told Dad he couldn't wait to head to golf lessons the next morning.

Hope had brought joy, and joy had many friends. Enemies of doubt and discouragement had been blown away.

Dad believed in him, and Ben didn't really care what the other kids thought anymore. With new courage, he realized it wasn't about his abilities, but about his attitude.

The next morning Ben whistled happily even when he missed his putts. The other kids tried to give him a hard time, but when he just laughed with them at himself, they realized it wasn't that much fun if he didn't react angrily. The Evil Scoundrel of Anger disliked losing this battle. Ben's angels, Yilt & Lontoo, did hula-hoops through golden heavenly rays.

"The Father's heart lived out through an earthly dad is powerful," said Yilt. "And God's purpose for this young lad is mighty," said Lontoo.

They continued their dance of praise to God and rejoiced in their part for bringing His kingdom from heaven to earth.

Chapter 6

Andy was having a great time learning water sports from Pops. He hadn't spent much time in the water except for a swimming pool in their neighborhood.

The ocean was a lot different. It was easier to float in salt water, but swimming was harder against the current, even if it was gentle. He didn't like the taste of the salt. He had tried stand-up paddle boarding, and his muscles were sore. Pops did it regularly to stay in shape. They usually saw dolphins nearby when they went early in the morning.

Andy wanted to try kayaking with Pops. He wasn't old enough to drive the jet ski, but he thought he could paddle his own kayak. Pops let him try on his own. Making the kayak move in the strong current was hard.

Andy decided it would be better to go in a tandem one with Pops. At first, he wasn't sure that he was helping Pops make the kayak move, but when Pops stopped steering in the back, Andy could feel that he was guiding the turns.

Pops taught him that it was important to paddle together, but he let Andy set the pace for how fast or slow they went. He was a little nervous about tipping over, and the wind made it hard to steer sometimes.

Pops took Andy toward the inland coastline. It was calm water and a great place to explore. Several times they saw moon jellyfish. Pops told Andy they don't have a brain. Andy didn't know if Pops was joking, but he didn't turn around. He thought he might tip the kayak over if he moved too much. He would have to ask him later.

"If you ever get stung by a jellie, pour vinegar on it. Vinegar keeps the poison from spreading and stops the pain." Andy knew Pops wasn't joking about this.

There were inlets with sea life and kelp forests that Andy would never have seen except from the kayak. Pops told Andy about these marine plants found in salt water.

"Kelp is a type of algae that grows tall in this area. Kelp doesn't have roots like trees; it has anchors that grip the rocks. It's called a forest because it grows close together like trees do in a forest on land. It's a safe zone for fish when they first hatch and during rough storms.

"I help with beach cleanup when I can. When the water warms up in the summer sun, the kelp dies and washes up along the sand."

Pops pointed it out to Andy. "The kelp and seaweed that collects on the beach is called wrack. Cleaning it up will get rid of the stinky smell it can cause and keep it from getting tangled up under boats and surfers."

Pops had brought his binoculars and was looking all around. "There have been a few times that I've seen sea otters here." Andy hoped he would see one.

As they gently paddled through the calm waters close to shore, several birds flew over them and landed. Andy couldn't tell the difference until Pops pointed out their beaks.

"A blue heron has a dagger-like bill, and the pelican has a long, blunt bill. Pelicans can plunge-dive from high above to catch fish. They have a pouch to keep the fish in; once they land they spill the water out before swallowing the fish."

Andy loved kayaking in the gentle water close to shore. Grins had wanted to pack a lunch for them, but Pops had just grabbed some apples. Andy was getting hungry and happily munched on his apple as they headed back to White Ferry Landing.

Pops suggested they should do some jet-skiing around the harbor when they got back from their kayak trip. He called Todd to ask if he wanted to bring the twins and join them.

As they docked the kayak, Pops saw Bailey waving to them from White Ferry Landing. He wondered if she would be scared to jet ski again.

Ben went first with his dad. Pops bounced over the water to come up beside them. Andy held on tight. It seemed like Pops was racing Todd and Ben. They were hoarse from shouting to each other over the loud motor. Andy laughed so hard his stomach hurt. He was having a great time!

Todd brought his jet ski to the dock and Ben got off to give Bailey a turn.

"Are you sure you want to do this, Bailey?" Dad asked with concern. "Yep!" she replied. "Let's go!"

Dad tried to take off slowly and stay away from waves that might scare her if they got bumpy. Bailey had her arms around his waist and held on tight. But she wasn't afraid.

She was enjoying the view of the harbor and the long bridge that went from the island to the mainland.

Todd was grateful for Bailey's fear being removed. He thanked God again for all He was doing in their lives. He knew there was one more

69

thing he needed to work on and prayed for help. God heard his prayer and was already bringing an answer.

The days were filled with jet-skiing and swimming. Andy was becoming good friends with Ben and Bailey. They rode their bikes to the park. They played beach volleyball and built sandcastles.

They all got up early one morning when it was low tide to go shelling. It had rained the night before, and the fog was so thick they couldn't see Point Crim Lighthouse.

The beach was full of purple and fuzzy sand dollars that morning. Some were still half buried in the sand.

Andy was amazed. He had never seen this many at one time. They stepped carefully through the sand, making sure they didn't disturb them. Bailey told him they were still alive if they were purple and moved. The kids watched as the beautiful creatures made a very, very slow visible path in the sand. "Look at this one," Andy shouted. "It looks like it's just a shell."

Bailey bent down to take a closer look. "It looks like it has fur. And the edges are still spiny. That means it is still alive and we shouldn't disturb it. The waves will take it back into the ocean."

There were other shells, too. "This one looks like angel wings." Andy picked up the shell. It was still connected, and Bailey giggled. "Those are hard to find with the wings still together. Way to go!"

Andy handed it to her. "I think you should have it," he said as he gave her the small shells.

Bailey thanked him. "I'd like to keep it as a special reminder." Ben gave her a questioning look. She still hadn't gotten to tell her brother all of the good things she experienced at camp.

The twins found several varieties of shells and used the Shell & Sea Creature Identifier book that Grins had given Bailey. "This one looks like a Cut Ribbed Ark. And this one looks like a Turkey Wing."

Ben was getting the pages wet as he flipped through the book. "Look, Bailey. There is a shell that's called an Angel Wing. It looks a little bit like the one we found, but that could be a clamshell, too." They all gathered around to look. Andy shrugged. "I can't tell the difference," he said.

They were headed toward the beautiful resort area where the big, craggy rocks held tiny crabs. The kids had brought their special shoes called water socks so they could carefully climb around the rocks and shallow tide pools. Bailey wanted to touch the coral, but she knew it could easily cut her fingers.

"What is this?" Andy asked. Bailey was learning a lot about sea life, but she checked the book to make sure it was an anemone.

Andy laughed at the funny sounding word. He had a hard time saying it without getting his tongue all twisted.

Suddenly they heard a scream. The kids hadn't realized there were other people following on the beach. They looked toward the water and saw a child with wildly flailing arms. Andy jumped down from the rocks and took off running in the sand. Bailey and Ben followed right behind him.

Andy began to pray as he ran. "What should I do, God?" Andy had learned that when he asked, God would show him what to do. Andy reached the screaming little girl just as her daddy did. He was frantic, and the little girl cried even more. No one knew what was wrong.

Andy prayed for God's peace and knelt down next to the stomping child. The water rushed in around them, and Andy almost lost his balance.

Angels were near; sent by God as an answer to Andy's prayer. At that moment, he knew what was wrong and what to do. "I think it's a jellyfish sting," he said, looking at the frustrated father. "Let's get her onto the sandy beach. I have something in my backpack that will help."

Andy pulled off his backpack and took out the small container of vinegar he had brought to clean shells. The father knelt in the sand and tried to comfort the little girl. "Rachel, calm down!" he yelled. But Rachel was kicking her legs and crying in pain.

"Hold her tightly," Andy told her father. "This is vinegar, and it will stop the toxins in the stingers from spreading."

The adults that had gathered around looked at him as if he was crazy, but Andy poured the vinegar over her right leg first. He didn't have a lot of the liquid and wanted to make sure which leg had been stung. The little girl began to calm down. She sniffled as she tried to reach her left leg to scratch.

When she stopped kicking, they could see the red welts on both of her legs. Andy poured vinegar over the red puffy area on the other leg. The little girl stopped crying.

"Does that help, Rachel?" her daddy asked. She nodded, and he wiped her tears with his hand.

"It's better now," she said, hugging his neck. He hugged her tightly and kissed her forehead.

"How did you know what was wrong?" the man asked Andy. He looked at his little girl's legs and saw the red marks left by the stinger. "I didn't know there were jellyfish here."

"When I pray, God helps me," he answered simply. "He loves your little girl and you so much. I think He gave me an answer for her."

Andy remembered Grins had insisted that he take a small bottle of vinegar in his backpack to clean the shells. He'd told her they could wait until they got back to the house to clean them, but she had insisted. It hadn't made sense to him until now.

"I wanted to clean up the ocean," the little girl said. "I was going to pick up a plastic bag I saw."

"That's it!" Bailey said, grasping Andy's arm. "Sometimes jellyfish look like a clear plastic wrapper. Did you see it? Is that how you knew?"

"I didn't see anything with my eyes, but I knew it with my heart. Listening for God's voice gives us a lot of helpful information." He looked at Bailey. "He's a really good father to us, just like this daddy is to his little girl. We can trust Him when we know Him."

Andy watched them walk from the beach. Rachel's daddy had been so thankful for his help. Andy was thankful, too. Pops had just told him about the vinegar for a jellie's stings, and it had been useful for this situation. He had become strong and courageous as he learned to hear God's voice more often. Using God's gifts to help others felt like an adventure. He thanked God for helping him know what to do and for the courage to speak up.

"I'm hungry," Bailey laughed. "I hope Dad will fix breakfast soon."

"Me, too," Andy said as they took off their water socks and wiggled their feet in the sand with each step.

They were quiet as they walked toward the empty lifeguard station. No one was in it this early. Ben finally asked the question he'd been wondering about. "Andy, how did you know about the jellyfish sting?"

Andy shrugged. It was like I told Rachel's dad, "I prayed and listened for God."

Ben tried to understand, but he didn't know if he believed that God would give a kid information to help him with things on earth.

"I used to be afraid of a lot of things. You could say I was pretty wimpy," Andy laughed. "But when I asked God to give me courage and began to pray and read the Bible more, I began to know His voice and His love. He wants to be our friend and our father. Knowing Him makes us strong and wise. We're here on earth to bring His power and goodness to those around us."

Ben didn't know what to say, but he wanted to be strong and powerful. He hadn't thought that God would make that kind of difference in his life. He changed the subject. "My friends are surfing later this morning if you want to join us."

Bailey and Andy both yelled, "Sure!" at the same time. Ben laughed.

"The waves should be good today. Once the sun breaks through the fog, it would be fun." Ben said it, but in his heart, he was still upset about that first day out on the water.

"Someone will have to give me some lessons," Andy said, looking from Ben to Bailey. "I've learned to Boogie Board, and I'm pretty good at stand-up paddle boarding, but I'm ready to learn surfing. Maybe Pops will come."

He didn't know Pops' schedule. The parade was in a few days, and Andy knew he was getting the Mustang ready.

Bailey took off her backpack and pulled out some cherries. Andy grinned. "You know what we do with those in my cousins' family? We have a spitting contest to see who can spit the seed the farthest."

"You're on!" Ben said grabbing a handful of cherries. Bailey handed a few to Andy, and they made a line in the sand. After chewing the cherry and making sure only the seed was left in their mouth, Andy counted down with his fingers. Three, two, one! Blast! The seeds went flying. They ran to look for the landing spot of each.

Bailey picked something up, but it wasn't her seed. It was something mushy a bird had left behind. "Yuck!" Bailey ran back to the water to wash her fingers.

"Let's try again," Ben said. They each took a cherry and chewed down to the seed. Three, two, one! They spit again, and Andy's seed almost hit someone coming towards them. It was Pops!

"No need to be spitting at me," Pops said, laughing. "But I'll take on all three of you! I'm pretty sure I have more practice and skill at this than all of you put together."

Sure enough, Pops won the spitting contest every round after that. They finally had all the cherries they could hold, and Pops said he had come to see if Andy was ready for some surfing lessons. Andy grinned. "Yes!" he said, looking around for the board.

"I thought you would want breakfast first," Pops said. "Grins is baking cinnamon rolls. If you're not too full of cherries, you can all eat with us this morning."

When they headed back to the beach, Grins had her camera ready, and Pops had promised to help Andy. They waxed their boards, pulled on wetsuits and walked through the sand toward the crashing waves.

Ben and Bailey headed towards the bigger waves. Ben asked Bailey if she was okay with the water. Bailey finally got to tell Ben about her experience with Sara at camp.

"That's great!" Ben was happy for his twin sister although he didn't understand all that she was talking about. He was impressed as she surfed beside him.

"I learned that the beginning point of the wave is the peak and the end is the shoulder. The best waves go parallel to the beach. As the waves break at the end, there's a channel of water that gets you back into the rip to get you back out into the lineup." Bailey laughed. "It's like a big circle of riding waves."

Ben was impressed. "You did learn a lot at Surf Camp, and it shows." She was doing really good with paddling and jumping onto the board. Her position was good, and she was able to stay ahead of the breaking water.

Andy watched them and sighed. He was trying to be patient as Pops insisted he practice on the sand first. He placed his body and hands on the board like Pops showed him.

He repeated the instructions. "Spring up, stay low, position feet." Finally, Pops agreed to take him into the water. The things he learned in the sand were helpful as he began to jump up on the surfboard and ride the breaking waves.

Andy had to concentrate to put all the things he was learning together and stay balanced on his board. Pops stayed next to him on his longboard. *Pops still rips like he is a young man.*

Andy remembered riding on his shoulders when he was very little. That had let Andy feel how fantastic surfing could be, but he had to do it on his own now that he was older. He knew practicing more often was what he needed.

He wanted to keep going, but his body needed a break. He knew Pops had plans for the three of them that afternoon.

Chapter 7

That afternoon, the kids hopped into Pops' jeep, and he took them up the winding road to Point Crim Lighthouse. Although it was no longer used to show ships where to go, it was open daily for tours. Visitors could walk through it and ask a tour guide questions. Many people chose to walk to the edge of the cliffs and view the beautiful ocean below.

It wasn't a tall building since it was located at the top of the cliffs overlooking the ocean. Pops told the kids that because it was set so high up, fog and clouds were sometimes lower than the tower. Ships could not see the beacon light when it was above the fog and thick clouds.

He pointed towards the tower. "It's been said, that on foggy nights, the lighthouse keeper would have to use a shotgun for noise to warn ships away from the rocky cliffs below."

At first, Andy thought Pops was joking, but he could tell by the look on his face that he was serious. "Wow," Andy said. "Just wow!"

The tower's bottom level looked like rooms of a house. Pops explained that a lighthouse had been the home of the lighthouse keeper and his family, and they had to make sure there were plenty of supplies to keep the light burning every night.

As Ben and Andy explored the small rooms, they got to see what family life was like for lighthouse keepers. The kitchen and dining room were combined, and a little bedroom was on the side. Another room was for storing food and supplies.

Bailey climbed the circling stairway to the top. She read a sign about how the lamps and glass were kept clean. She wondered if it was a lonely life so far away from any other people.

What she didn't see were the many angels who were assigned to this place that had often alerted sailors of danger. God's angels brought protection and peace to the hearts of the lonely families. These families helped others by shining a beacon of light into the storms to keep them safe.

Andy asked how the light could shine without electricity. "Good question," Pops replied. "Light came from something like a large oil lamp's flame in those early days. Whale oil and kerosene were used then. There would be a lantern room with glass all around it for the lamp. The light from that flame had to be focused by a special lens around it so it could shine for a very long distance."

Ben wanted to know if a lighthouse was still useful with all the technology there is now. Pops nodded. "Another good question. It's like a backup system to use buoys in the water and a lighthouse on land," he explained. "The purpose of a lighthouse was to let ships know their location and to warn boats of dangerous rocks in the area. It was sort of like a traffic signal to ships on the sea."

They could tell Pops loved the Island's history and the kids loved his stories. Andy realized his grandfather's stories were a great benefit to everyone who came on a tour.

They finished their tour and took some pictures. Bailey wanted to text a picture of the three of them to Mom. This view of the Island beach made it look small. She couldn't wait to tell Mom the stories and history she was learning. It was still hard to be away from her mom, and she had hoped that Mom and Dad would get back together.

On their way back, Pops took them to the Cupcakery Shoppe. It was his favorite sweet treat.

Andy picked Peppermint Patty, a mint chocolate cupcake with vanilla frosting. Ben asked for the Breakfast PB and J that was chocolate with peanut butter chips. It had bacon bits in the peanut butter and jelly frosting.

Bailey looked at Pops. "I'll try your favorite," she said. "What is it?"

Pops laughed. "I have a lot of favorites. I think you might like the Snoring S'mores one."

Her eyes widened. "I do love s'mores around a campfire. I'll try it!" It was chocolate cake with marshmallow filling, topped with chocolate ganache and crushed graham crackers.

All four were quiet as they ate the cupcakes. Pops asked Bailey about her time at the camp. When she told them about Jackson's prayer, Ben interrupted her. "I asked God to keep Mom and Dad from separating, and it didn't happen. I don't think He always hears me."

Pops nodded. "Sometimes it seems like that, Ben, when we don't get what we want. God always hears us. But He's not a magician. He allows people to choose and sometimes we don't like the choices they make."

Andy looked at his new friend. "I'm sorry that happened to your family, Ben. God promises to always be with us, but I think it would be tough to have your family situation."

Bailey nodded. "It is hard. They both love us and we love them. I'm trying to be thankful for the good things we do have." Jeray and Bistoe danced for joy at God's goodness in her life. She was already learning His ways and making good choices.

Pops smiled at her. "You are a courageous young lady and I'm proud of your attitude. I believe you are going to be a lot like the lighthouse we just toured."

Bailey didn't understand, and Pops explained. "Your kind words are like a light to others, and that light will show them the right way to go."

Bailey smiled. She wanted to be helpful to others.

Pops' phone rang. He looked at the phone and then winked at the kids. "I'm in trouble!" He laughed as he picked up the phone.

"You caught me!" he said. "I'm having cupcakes with the kids." They could hear Grins' laughter on the phone. She was calling to remind him that Andy's parents would be arriving soon.

Andy was happy that his mom and dad were coming. He hoped Dad would watch him surf tomorrow. They hadn't gotten to surf together and Andy knew his dad was good at it. Mom would love watching them. He could hardly wait.

The next morning Andy was awakened by a siren on their street. He looked out the window and saw an ambulance go past. He silently prayed for the people who were in need, and the EMT's who were going to help. He asked God to give the first responders wisdom and courage and to bring His goodness and healing to those they were helping.

Andy knew that some of his friends thought it was silly to pray about everything, but they hadn't seen miracle answers like he had. He prayed that they would. The first time he had prayed for someone's headache to go away, he had been shy. But when the pain immediately left her, he stopped worrying and knew it was worth an awkward moment.

He remembered little Rachel and thanked God again for helping him to know it was a jellyfish sting, having the vinegar with him, and knowing what to do.

Pops knocked on Andy's door and asked if he wanted to go jet-skiing. *Yes!* He jumped out of bed and got dressed in a flash. He was excited that Mom and Dad were going, too.

Grins walked with them to White Ferry Landing and had her camera ready. Pops took Andy on his jet-ski, and his dad took his mom.

The water was cold, but Andy loved bouncing over the waves created by the wake of boats coming and going in the harbor. Mom was laughing and holding Dad tightly. It was her first-time jet-skiing and Andy thought she was having fun.

When Pops finally came to the shore and let Andy off, his lips were blue and he was shivering. Mom got off, too, and threw him a beach towel to wrap up in. He sat down next to Grins and her camera. Dad and Pops returned the jet-skis.

The adults got coffee from The Landing Coffee Shop and Andy warmed up with some hot chocolate. He knew Mom and Dad were wanting to go home today, but Pops had talked them into staying until after the parade tomorrow. Andy was thankful. He really wanted Dad to watch him surf.

Surfing didn't go as well as Andy wished it would have, but Dad encouraged him to keep trying. He watched as his dad and grandfather seemed to glide over the waves. He hoped to be that good at surfing someday.

Andy remembered how he used to be miserable if someone was better at something than he was. He knew he had choices and that choosing to find the good things made him feel better and helped him to have more fun. When he spent more time thinking about good things, his mind didn't have room for anything else to stay there.

He sat on the beach to take a break. Just then Ben and Bailey brought their surfboards to join the fun. Todd brought his board but wanted to watch his kids from the shore. Andy's dad went to sit with Grins.

Andy decided to try again, and Pops sat next to Todd on the beach. "These days remind me of when your dad and I were growing up here," Pops said.

Todd looked surprised. "You and my dad were good friends?"

Pops nodded. "We lived next door and did a lot together, although he was a few years older than I. He left one summer to surf the world and I left to farm the Plains."

Todd was watching with amazement as Bailey surfed. *She was beginning to do cut-backs!* He was amazed. Making an S shape with a surfboard on a wave took skill.

"Great job!" He jumped up from the sand and cheered. He looked at Pops. "She's changed since camp," he said. "Not just her surfing skills, but her attitude and everything. She's made me want to have a relationship with God again. I'm just not sure where to start. I feel like I let Him down by not talking with Him for so long."

Pops looked at him. "When your dad was the captain of his ship, you could go there anytime. Everything on the ship was open to you because you were his son. That's how God is with His children. What's His, is available to us. Because we belong to Him, we can freely ask Him anything. Start with knowing how much He loves you. When you believe that, you'll talk with Him about everything."

"Thanks." Todd nodded. He watched Ben and Bailey. *They were doing great.* He just wanted to be out there with them. "Sorry to leave you, Pops. I want to go be with my kids."

Pops motioned for Todd to go. "Enjoy these moments!" Pops was happy to watch the three of them. The angels were full of joy as they watched the beings on earth act like their heavenly Father towards His children - just wanting to be with them because He loved them.

Andy's dad, Paul, came back to join them. His mom, Lisa, cheered and waved as he tried and fell. Andy sighed. He was trying to be patient. He watched his friends doing better and tried not to compare. He'd been afraid of too many things in the past, and although trying new things was hard, he knew he was much more courageous than before.

Pops walked back to where Grins was taking videos. "I'm going to get some fishing gear together. Ben and Todd have a tee time for golf, but Bailey wants to do some fishing with us. You wanna come along?"

He was teasing her and she knew it. "Thanks, but I'd rather eat worms!" Pops raised his eyebrows. "Wow!" They both laughed.

"Maybe I should take videos. I guess I will come along. Someone needs to record these moments." Grins hopped up and brushed off the sand. She didn't like fishing at all, but she didn't want to miss out.

"We could take the ferry across and try fishing off the pier again. Maybe we can catch some yellowfin croaker and get Todd to make more of those fish tacos," Pops said.

Grins clapped and shouted a rather loud "Woo Hoo!" She loved fish tacos, especially if someone else did the cooking.

Andy's parents decided to stay on the beach and relax in the sun.

When the kids finished surfing, they stood in a circle with their boards on the beach. They were anxious to get out of their wetsuits. It had been a great morning and the waves were nearly perfect.

Todd and Ben had to hurry to make their tee time. Bailey wanted the first shower and Ben reminded her that he was in a hurry. They began to argue.

Andy interrupted them with a joke. "Knock-knock," he said. The twins stared at him.

"Fine," Bailey said. I'll go along with your joke. Who's there?" "Etch," Andy grinned. "Etch who?" Bailey replied. "Bless you!" Andy said, laughing.

Ben groaned. "Dumb joke," but he was smiling.

"Knock-knock," Andy said again.

This time Ben responded. "Who's there?"

"Andy," Andy said. The twins gave him a funny look.

"Okay. Andy who?" Bailey said.

"And he sneezed again," Andy laughed. Ben and Bailey laughed, too. The silly jokes made them forget their argument.

Bailey looked at Ben. "You can go first, Ben. I'll help Andy put the boards up."

Andy and Bailey walked to the back of the house where Pops kept his surfboards stacked. Andy was quiet. Bailey told him she was thinking about her choices and how they affected the people she loved most. Their angels were all around, cheering for the courage of these humans.

Ben was happy to be golfing with his dad. When they were paired with two older men, he felt annoyed. *Why can't I just have time alone with my dad?* As they each drove their first ball off the tee, he realized he was better than either of the men, and they complimented his great swing.

Dad had helped him improve the distance he could drive the ball. He was taking his time angling his putts, and his score showed it. He was happy that he had listened to Dad's instructions so carefully. Ben was grateful that Dad was more patient in teaching him, too.

Not only did they have a great game, but the men treated him and Dad to burgers at the Clubhouse afterward. *Not so bad after all.*

Andy loved the ferry ride across the bay, but fishing was a bust. Nothing was biting, and he got tired of waiting. Catching grunion in the sand had been better. Andy felt grumpy. He looked at the others. No one else seemed to be having a good time either. Except for Grins. She was videoing everyone being grumpy.

Bailey clapped when Pops said he was done with fishing off the pier. "You'll have to go to the grocery store if we eat fish tonight," Pops said, looking at Grins. She just nodded and laughed.

"Let's get back to the ferry," she said to Bailey. They started along the boardwalk while Pops and Andy picked up the tackle and bait. He carried the net and Pops took the poles.

Ben was surprised when they got back to the house before Bailey. He was glad to get some time with just Dad. Dad asked Ben if he wanted to watch the baseball game on T.V. *Best day ever. Surfing, golfing and now watching baseball with Dad.*

Ben got a text from Tony, asking him to surf the next day. He'd planned to ride in the parade in Pops' Mustang. He knew Bailey and Andy would be disappointed if he didn't.

Ben had to make a choice. He really needed the practice time in the water, but he couldn't do both. He decided to talk to Dad about it. He really liked Dad's new way of handling things. Ben could trust his advice and began to feel more peaceful.

When Dad told Ben it would be fine for him to choose surfing, Ben was happy. When Dad asked if he could come, too, Ben nearly fell out of his chair.

Chapter 8

The day of the parade started off with a thunderstorm and a shower of rain. Ben loved it. He knew that the storm brought great waves for surfing. The decision to surf with Tony and Garth and Dad would be more exciting than getting wet in the parade.

Andy was disappointed that Ben chose to surf instead of joining them in the Mustang for the parade. Sometimes having two fun choices was as hard as having tough choices. He prayed about it and chose not to let the Evil Scoundrel of Jealousy sneak into his heart.

The Crimson Island parade was held every summer and ended at the beach where there was food and bounce houses and games for all ages. The surfers carrying their boards behind their old woody wagon car came first. Next were a few old tractors and two covered wagons pulled by horses.

The floats from several schools were colorful and filled with kids. Grins told Andy that the schoolchildren and the folks from the retirement community had worked together to make the floats. She pointed out the one that she and Pops had helped with. One of the students waved wildly to get her attention. Grins waved back and told Andy that she had also helped the little girl learn to read better when they met after school each week.

When it was time for the old cars, Bailey and Andy sat in the back seat of the Mustang and took turns tossing pieces of candy into the crowd. Bailey recognized several friends she had met at Surf Camp and threw bubble gum their way. It was her favorite and she wanted to share it.

The car behind them had a loud and annoying horn. Every time it honked, Bailey jumped!

They liked waving at the crowd on both sides of the street. Andy missed not seeing the marching bands from the sidelines, but he was having too much fun feeling like a celebrity as he waved to the folks watching.

Several kids on skateboards flew past them. Andy realized he could have done that, too. *Maybe next year?* He remembered Mom and Dad talking about moving. He sighed. He wanted to know the future, and he didn't want to move. Andy knew God would be with him and help him be strong and courageous no matter what their decision was.

When they reached the end of the parade route, Andy saw his parents were already at the beach. Dad was helping set up a silly game called Dangling Donuts.

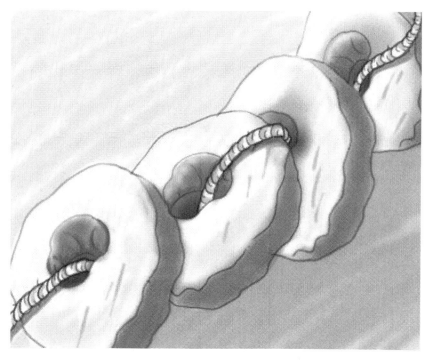

They'd already removed the nets from the volleyball poles and tied a clean, white rope between them. Four donuts would be hung on each end. There was a contest to see which side could eat the fastest. Their hands would be tied with a kerchief behind their back.

Andy's dad had a timer, and each contestant had an entrance number next to their name. If the donut fell off the rope, the player was done. Every set of players got a clean white rope for their four donuts.

There were plain, jelly-filled and frosted. It was a messy game, but a favorite of all. The winner would get a year's supply of free donuts from the Island Bakery store.

Andy decided to be a contestant. He thought that if he won the prize, he could give it as a gift to Pops. Pops and his sweet tooth would love that! He got his number and waited nearby.

Bailey saw Andy signing up and decided to enter, too. The two of them were paired against each other, and their numbers were called first.

When the starting pop sounded, Andy got on his knees and bit into the first donut. He was glad his hands were tied behind his back because it was tempting to use them to keep the donuts from falling off the rope.

Bailey got under the rope and ate from the bottom. It worked well, and she finished her first donut faster than Andy.

The second one Andy bit into was filled with ooey-gooey jelly and it ran down his chin and onto his shirt. He didn't take time to see how Bailey was doing but kept his focus on the donut and his mouth. The last bite looked like it would fall and

Andy moved his cheek to hold it on the rope while he chewed the rest of the donut and tried not to move his face. He missed a piece of the last bite and it fell to the ground, but he just kept going.

His stomach was starting to hurt because he was so full and was eating so fast. He heard a roar from the crowd and wondered if Bailey had beat him.

He didn't stop. He tried to eat faster and almost choked as he took bigger bites to finish the last donut. His face was covered with chocolate frosting as he jumped up and made a mumbling noise while trying to yell that he was finished and not spew the mess from his mouth at the same time.

The crowd cheered again. He looked over to see if Bailey was done. She was wiping the frosting from her face with the kerchief that was used to tie her hands. She raised her hands with the messy kerchief as she began jumping and cheering. Everyone watching them was shouting and laughing.

Andy was bummed that Bailey had beat him, but he clapped for her and went to give her a congratulatory handshake. Andy's dad wrote down their times and called the number for the next players.

Andy's mom helped to set up the next clean rope and hang the donuts in their spots. The line of people wanting to join the contest had gotten very long.

Bailey and Andy went to the outdoor water stations that had been set up to clean themselves. Bailey looked at Andy. "That might not have been such a good idea. I think I might puke," she said.

Andy nodded. "Let's sit down under an umbrella and take it easy for a bit."

They watched as the line of people tried to eat donuts faster and faster. Several donuts dropped off the rope, and that person was out. The fastest times were within a few seconds when suddenly they heard the crowd roar louder.

They saw a man wearing a yellow shirt. "He's last year's winner," they heard someone say. People pushed in close to watch as the starting pop went off again.

"Unbelievable," Pops said as he walked in behind Bailey and Andy. "I'm not even going to try to outdo that guy." Pops shook his head. Andy looked at him and put his hand on his stomach. "It's probably a good choice, Pops," he said, groaning.

Pops laughed as he looked at Andy's miserable face. "It looks like you already tried this," he said.

"I did. Bailey beat me." Andy looked at Pops. "I would have given the prize to you. It was a year's worth of donuts."

Pops laughed harder. "And you'd have gotten me in big trouble with Grins for eating too many sweets!" They all laughed. They knew it was true.

"She's one of the best things God has brought into my life," he said, his tone serious. "Someone who helps you make good choices is a gift."

The line for donut eating had slowed down. The seagulls were trying to get close enough to pick up the pieces left in the sand.

Just then Ben, his dad and Tony walked up behind Bailey and shouted her name. Bailey jumped and playfully swatted at Ben. "You scared me," she giggled.

"That was my goal," Ben laughed.

"Well, you missed the entertainment! I beat Andy in the Dangling Donut contest." Bailey enjoyed seeing her brother's surprised look. As they were teasing each other, their dad walked up to them and pointed at his phone.

"I'm going home for a bit," Dad said, looking serious. He turned and walked away before they could answer. The twins looked at each other. Ben shrugged. "Probably work. He's always working."

"Things have been different lately, Ben," Bailey said quietly. Ben smiled and put his arm around her shoulder. "You should have seen me surfing the waves today," he told her.

"Yea, he did his best ripping ever," Tony said, giving Ben a high five.

"I'm sorry I missed it, but I had a great time in the parade." Bailey wiggled away from him. "You're wet," she said.

"And you have chocolate in your hair," Ben shot back.

Andy's parents turned over their spot at the game table so the Island Bakery owners could announce the winner. Everyone knew it would be the man in the yellow shirt.

"It's time for us to get going," Andy's dad said. "We're going to walk back and get the car. Do you want to wait for us here or come back to the house, Andy?"

Andy looked at Ben and Bailey. He had to say goodbye to his new friends. He decided to walk back to the house.

"I want to get back to the house and see what's going on with Dad," Bailey said.

Ben nodded. He poked Andy's arm and laughed. "You're going to miss the Beach Cleanup tomorrow morning. You never know what kind of treasures you'll find with the seaweed!"

It felt sad to leave the Island, and Andy wished he could stay. He would gladly help clean the beach, but he missed his friends back home, too.

After telling Andy good-bye, the twins walked up to their house. The door was open and they could hear Dad talking on the phone.

"It sounds like he's talking to Mom," Bailey said, motioning for Ben to stop. She didn't want to listen when she shouldn't, but she had been praying for both of her parents, and this conversation sounded nicer than usual.

"Let's give him a few more minutes," she said, closing the door and motioning for Ben to sit with her on the front steps.

"What has been the best thing about your summer, Ben?" Bailey asked. Ben was quiet and Bailey let him have time to think about it.

"I wanted to do better at surfing, but that first time out something happened."

Bailey looked at him. He always seemed so confident, but something was bothering him. She let him finish.

"I think a dolphin got too close. I panicked and thought I was dying. It really scared me and I've had a hard time since then. I don't know if I'll ever be good enough to do competitions." Ben seemed sad.

There was so much to be thankful for and Bailey wanted to help Ben think about the good things. She asked God to help her. "You're good at a lot of things," she said. "I'm so happy we can surf together now that I'm not afraid anymore."

Yilt and Lontoo came close. Ben began to think about his new friend, Andy. He was the kindest friend he'd ever had. He remembered Dad's help with golf. That had certainly been a nice thing. He thought about the beach and all the fun he'd had. He laughed.

"What?" Bailey asked.

"I was just remembering Andy's dumb knock-knock jokes!" Bailey joined his laughter. Joy took over and sadness disappeared.

"Let's ride over to White Ferry Landing," Bailey said. Ben nodded, and they got their bikes out of the newly-cleaned garage.

As Andy's family prepared to leave, Pops asked them to join in a circle and pray together. Andy thanked God for his new friends as the angels rejoiced with him.

Mom thanked God for Grins and Pops and their love that reached out to neighbors and friends on the Island. The angels danced with joy at her thankful heart.

Dad thanked God for the ocean and the beach and the great time they had together. The angels worshipped and praised the Creator of the world.

Grins had tears in her eyes as she prayed for protection and safety as their family drove home. Angels of protection were ready and responded, as God answered her prayer.

Pops prayed a blessing over each of them and asked God to help them hear His voice more clearly in their hearts.

The angels cheered as the humans on earth said Amen together. They knew how important these moments on earth were for eternity.

Andy couldn't wait to ask his parents if they had decided to move. Dad's answer wasn't what he wanted to hear. "We are still praying about it, Andy. We know that God will show us step by step if this new job is right for our family and me."

His mom agreed. "We know God will show us. It would mean we would live closer to Grins and Pops. And closer the beach." She laughed as Andy whooped for joy.

"We're also making plans with Grins and Pops to all go back to the farm for Christmas this year."

Whoa! That was great news. Andy would love to see his cousin Annie and her little brother Adam. Uncle Jake and Aunt Liz were special to him, too. Maybe there would be ice skating on the neighbor's pond and snowball fights.

Andy's mind began whirring with excitement. God always had good things for him even when there were unknowns in his future. He would trust God with whatever was to come.

Andy hoped to make the soccer team at school this year. *What if we have to move? Will I get to play at a new school?* His anxious thoughts wanted to take over, and Andy knew he had a choice to make. Trust God or worry. He began to remember the good things in his life and asked God to give him peace.

The next morning Ben and Bailey were up early. It was their last day at the beach before they were going back to Mom's house. They wanted to get in one last morning of surfing. The dolphins were doing their graceful swim back and forth. Bailey stopped and dug her toes into the soft sand. Ben asked her what was wrong.

"Nothing is wrong," she told him. "I just wanted to enjoy the sand and watch the dolphins for a moment. It's not something I get to do when we're back with Mom."

Ben sighed and nodded. "I know," he said, quietly. "I miss Mom so much, and I miss our friends. But I love life here with Dad, too. Sometimes I get angry at them for making our lives complicated."

Bailey agreed. "We've talked about this before, Ben, and it doesn't get better. We'll get used to it. We can't solve the situation, but we can pray."

"What are you praying to happen, Bailey? Do you think they would ever get back together?" Ben wanted to be hopeful.

"We could pray together. The Bible says there's power in agreeing together when we pray." Bailey was hoping Ben would join her and bowed her head. The angels came near and brought hope to their hearts.

The surf was spectacular that morning, and the beach was full of people. The angels were all around, doing what God had assigned to them.

Ben concentrated on his duck dives and felt a new peace around him instead of fear. He was so happy to have Bailey surfing with him. When Ben got hungry, he called to Bailey that he wanted to go back to the house.

As the twins walked up to their house, Dad was waiting on the front porch to meet them. They looked at his grin and then each other. *Something was up.* Dad asked them to put their boards away so he could talk with them. Although they were anxious to get out of their wetsuits, they couldn't wait to hear what Dad had to say.

"Your mother and I have been talking. A lot. I'm going to take you back and have dinner with her tonight. God has been working in both of our hearts, and we want to work on our relationship." Dad's eyes were watering and he wiped them with the back of his hand.

Ben's eyes were wide as he looked at Dad and then at Bailey. "We just prayed about that," Ben said with wonder.

"That would be fantastic!" Bailey jumped up and down and ran to hug her dad.

Dad motioned for Ben to join them and hugged them both. "It might be an adventure for all of us," he said, laughing and crying at the same time. "One thing for sure. Your mom can't wait to see you both. As soon as you can pack your things, we'll get on the road."

"While you get ready, I'm going to go over to tell Grins and Pops. I'm sure they will be happy to look after the house here until I come back. I hope we will all come back together." Dad was as excited as the twins were.

The angels were in party mode, knowing that restored relationships were what God, the good Father wanted for humans. They knew when those on earth had faith and hope in Him their lives would be better.

As Grins and Pops waved goodbye to their neighbors' car, they took hands and thanked God for His goodness and all He was doing in the lives of the people they loved.

He has put his angels in charge of you to watch over you wherever you go.

Psalm 91:11

About the Author - Nadine Helmuth Patton loves the supernatural realm that comes from God and bringing His kingdom purposes to the next generation through stories of His goodness.

The beach is one of her favorite places to vacation. Nadine and her husband, Gary, live in Phoenix, Arizona and enjoy gardening and hosting parties in their home. They have 2 children and 5 grandchildren. She enjoys making their family time together an adventure.

She is the author of Angels on Assignment, Adventures on the Farm.

You can connect with her at: thehearteyes.com

Ashley Burgess is a talented artist and has been drawing from a very young age. She is extremely versatile and has recently focused her media in black and white portraits and digital calligraphy.

Ashley enjoys spending her free time riding her motorcycles, all of which have a name. Ashley makes her home in Arlington, Kansas.

Made in the USA
Monee, IL
12 November 2019